Discovering Special Cultures

商務印書館(香港)有限公司
http://www.commercialpress.com.hk

Australia • Brazil • Japan • Korea • Mexico • Singapore • Spain • United Kingdom • United States

Discovering Special Cultures 世界生活丰采

香港特別版由Heinle, a part of Cengage Learning 及商務印書館（香港）有限公司聯合出版。
This special Hong Kong edition is co-published by Heinle, a part of Cengage Learning, and The Commercial Press (H.K.) Ltd.

Director of Content Development:
Anita Raducanu
Series Editor: Rob Waring
Editorial Manager: Bryan Fletcher

Associate Development Editors:
Victoria Forrester, Catherine McCue
責任編輯：黃家麗

出版：

商務印書館（香港）有限公司
香港筲箕灣耀興道3號東匯廣場8樓

Cengage Learning
Units 808-810, 8th floor,
Tins Enterprises Centre,
777 Lai Chi Kok Road, Cheung Sha Wan,
Kowloon, Hong Kong

網址：http://www.commercialpress.com.hk

http://www.cengageasia.com

發行：香港聯合書刊物流有限公司
香港新界大埔汀麗路36號中華商務
印刷大廈3字樓

印刷：中華商務彩色印刷有限公司
版次：2010年3月 第1版第2次印刷

ISBN: 978-962-07-1875-5

出版説明

本館一向倡導優質閱讀，近年連續推出以“Q”為標誌的優質英語學習系列*(Quality English Learning)*，其中《Black Cat 優質英語階梯閱讀》，讀者反應令人鼓舞，先後共推出超過60本。

為進一步推動閱讀，本館引入Cengage 出版之*Footprint Library*，使用*National Geographic*的圖像及語料，編成百科英語階梯閱讀系列，有別於Black Cat 古典文學閱讀，透過現代真實題材，百科英語語境能幫助讀者認識今日的世界各事各物，擴闊視野，提高認識及表達英語的能力。

本系列屬non-fiction (非虛構故事類)讀本，結合閱讀、視像和聽力三種學習功能，是一套三合一多媒介讀本，每本書的英文文章以headwords寫成，headwords 選收自以下數據庫的語料：*Collins Cobuild The Bank of English*、*British National Corpus* 及 *BYU Corpus of American English* 等，並配上精彩照片，另加一張video/audio 兩用DVD。編排由淺入深，按級提升，只要讀者堅持學習，必能有效提高英語溝通能力。

商務印書館(香港)有限公司
編輯部

使用說明

百科英語階梯閱讀分四級，共八本書，是彩色有影有聲書，每本有英語文章供閱讀，根據數據庫如 *Collins Cobuild The Bank of English*、*British National Corpus* 及 *BYU Corpus of American English* 選收常用字詞編寫，配彩色照片及一張video/audio 兩用DVD，結合閱讀、聆聽、視像三種學習方式。

讀者可使用本書：

學習新詞彙，並透過延伸閱讀(Expansion Reading)
練習速讀技巧

聆聽錄音提高聽力，模仿標準英語讀音

看短片做練習，以提升綜合理解能力

Grammar Focus解釋語法重點，後附練習題，供讀者即時複習所學，書內其他練習題，有助讀者掌握學習技巧如 scanning, prediction, summarising, identifying the main idea

中英對照生詞表設於書後，既不影響讀者閱讀正文，又具備參考作用

Contents 目錄

The CD-ROM contains a video and full recording of the text

CD-ROM *包括短片和錄音*

Words to Know

This story is set in the United States. It happens in the state of Delaware.

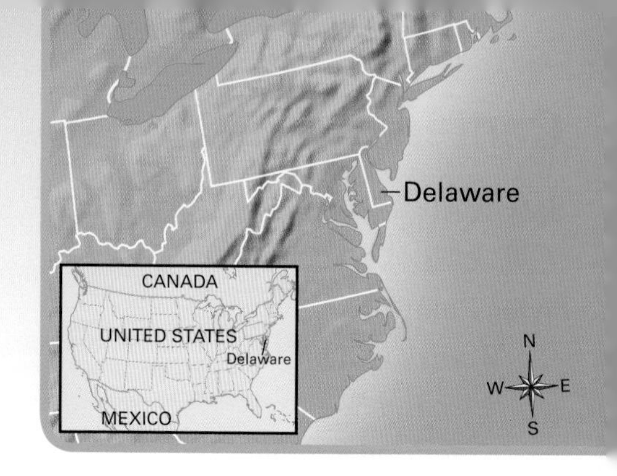

A Competition. Read the paragraph. Label the pictures with the correct form of the underlined words.

This story is about an unusual competition, or contest, between various teams. The winner in this contest is the team that throws a pumpkin farther than anyone else. The teams use different types of equipment and machines to throw the pumpkins. Some teams use a catapult to throw their pumpkin. Some teams use a cannon to blow their pumpkin through the air. One team even uses garage door springs and a kind of container called a bucket to get their pumpkin to fly. Before the contest, teams practise throwing many different things. They throw watermelons, kegs, and even refrigerators!

1. ____________ 2. ____________ 3. ____________

B **Weights and Measures.** In the story you will read about pounds to measure weight and feet to measure distance. What are these weights and distances in metric measures?

1 pound = .45 kilograms	1 foot = .31 metres

1. 8 pounds = __________ kilograms

2. 387 feet = __________ metres

3. 1,728 feet = __________ metres

4. __________

5. __________

6. __________

7. __________

8. __________

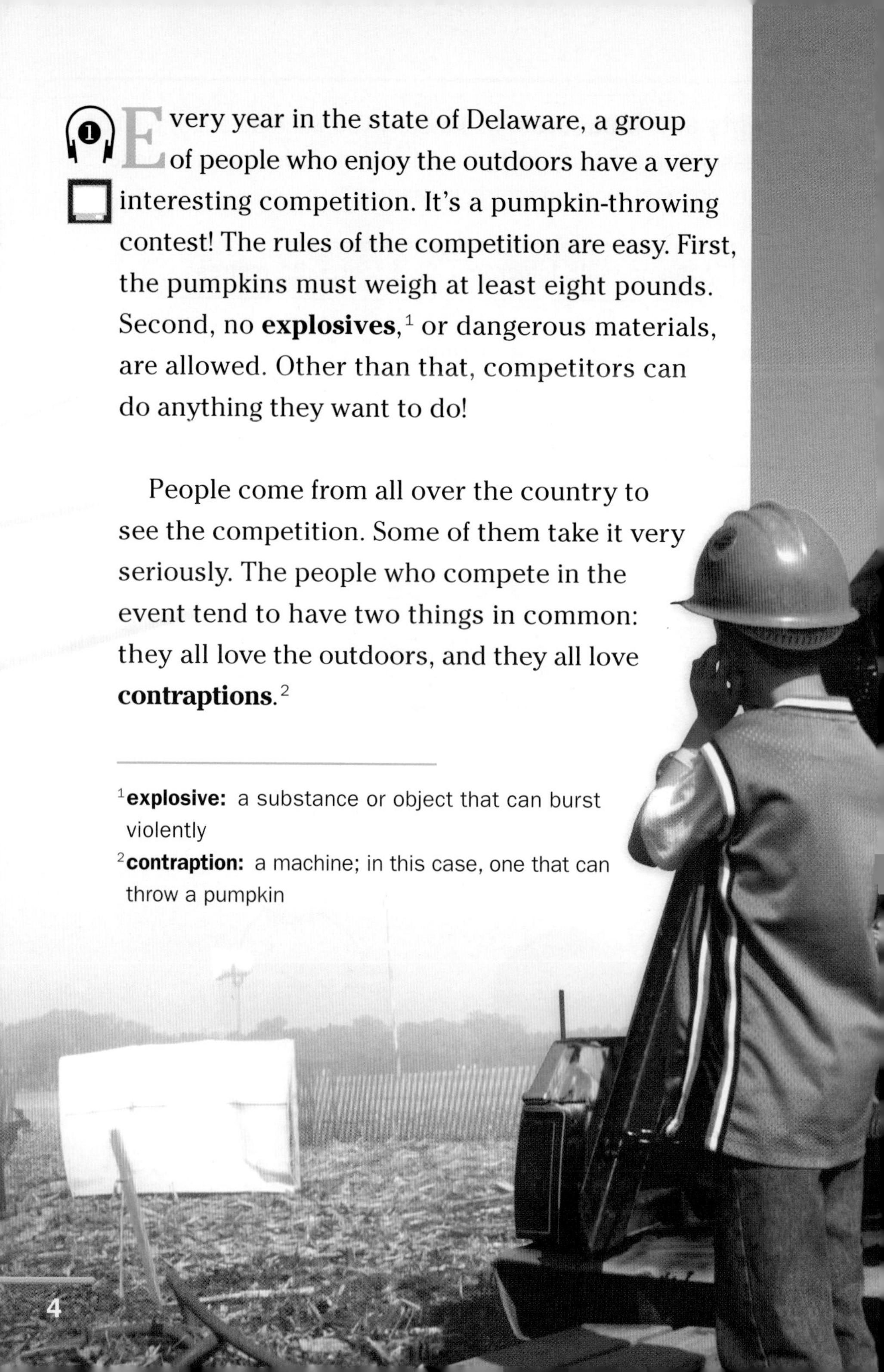

Every year in the state of Delaware, a group of people who enjoy the outdoors have a very interesting competition. It's a pumpkin-throwing contest! The rules of the competition are easy. First, the pumpkins must weigh at least eight pounds. Second, no **explosives**,[1] or dangerous materials, are allowed. Other than that, competitors can do anything they want to do!

People come from all over the country to see the competition. Some of them take it very seriously. The people who compete in the event tend to have two things in common: they all love the outdoors, and they all love **contraptions**.[2]

---

[1] **explosive:** a substance or object that can burst violently

[2] **contraption:** a machine; in this case, one that can throw a pumpkin

There are several teams that take part in the contest. Mick Davies is part of a group that has taken part in the competition for many years. Mick talks about his team, and how they've improved since they began. 'We started out with a little contraption with about 14 garage door springs on it,' he says. 'We threw 387 feet that first year – and we've **progressed**[1] from there.'

So what do they call this strange contest that keeps people coming back year after year?

[1]**progress:** to improve

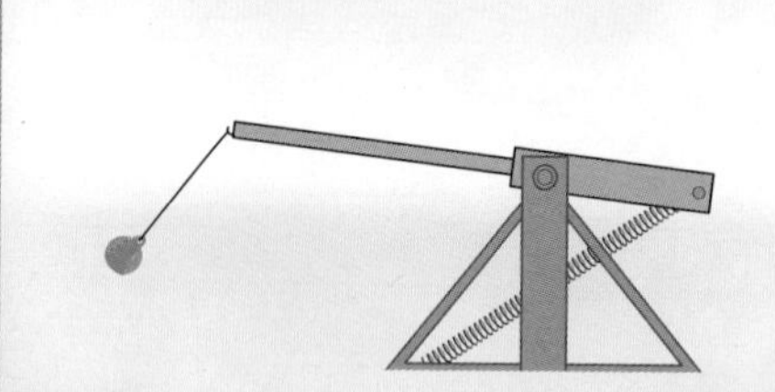

A Pumpkin-Throwing Contraption

This fun annual contest's unusual name is the '**Punkin' Chunkin'**[1] Contest.' The aim of the competition is simple: to make a machine that can throw a pumpkin through the air. The machine that throws – or chunks – a pumpkin the farthest wins. The teams make these contraptions themselves. They work hard to make **original**[2] machines that will chunk a pumpkin a long way.

Some women compete in the event, but not many. However, the contest does affect the men's wives – especially while the men prepare for the Punkin' Chunkin' Contest. One team member explains, 'The ladies that don't like to get involved, they know right around September ... October, that [it's] about time to become a Punkin' Chunkin' **widow**.'[3]

---

[1]**Punkin' Chunkin':** pumpkin throwing
[2]**original:** containing new ideas
[3]**widow:** a woman whose husband is dead

The unusual sport of Punkin' Chunkin' began over 20 years ago. In those days, there were only three teams and a few of their friends who came to watch. But now, more than 20 years later, this strange contest has really grown. It's become very popular. Today, the competition attracts more than 80 teams, and more than 20,000 people come to watch it!

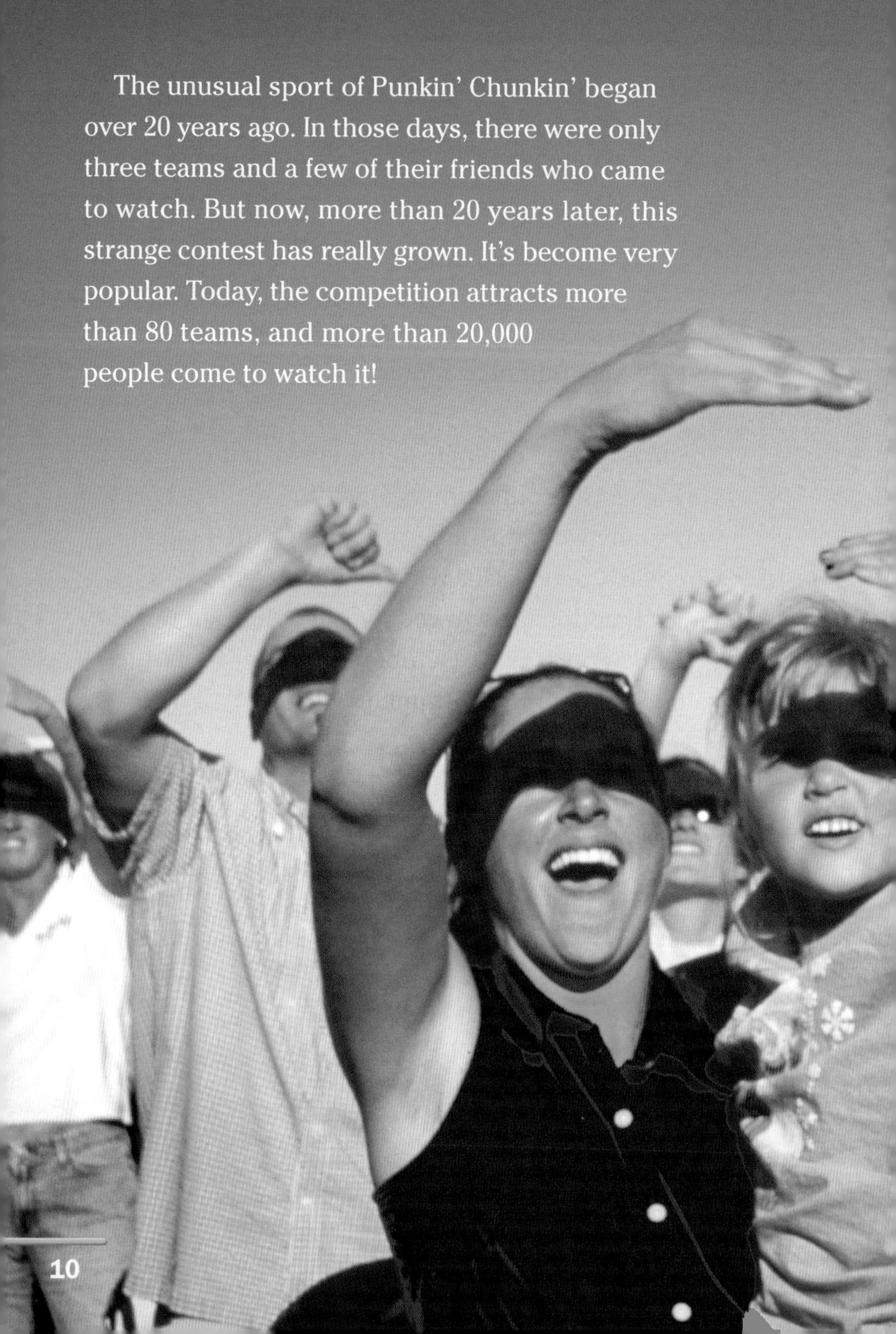

Fact Check

1. Where does the contest happen?
2. What is the contest called?
3. What is the goal of the contest?
4. When did it start?

In Punkin' Chunkin', the actual sport itself is not that difficult. However, people have to think carefully about the design of the machine if they want to win. All of the teams in the contest think that they've created just the right one. John Huber is a member of a team named 'Team Hypertension'. He talks about their machine: 'It's probably one of the few machines on this field that's really **engineered**,[1] so that we know **what it can take**[2] – every bit of it.' He goes on to say, 'I know what every **weld**[3] can hold. There isn't anything that's going to surprise us.'

Team Hypertension started seven years ago. It used garage door springs to throw its first pumpkin from a bucket. Since that time, the competition has become much more advanced.

---

[1]**engineer:** design or create something according to scientific methods
[2]**what it can take:** how much the machine can do
[3]**weld:** a part where metal is joined to metal

Nowadays, Punkin' Chunkin' machines can be anything from a simple **catapult**[1] to an actual **cannon**.[2] A good design isn't everything, though. If a team really wants to win, they need to practise. To do this, they throw many things, not just pumpkins. A member of one team explains: 'We chunk pumpkins, watermelons, kegs, toilets, refrigerators, **microwaves**,[3] tyres ... we chunk anything we can **get our hands on**!'[4] Unfortunately, even with a lot of practice, things don't always go perfectly. Accidents can still happen!

---

[1]**catapult:** a device for throwing objects
[2]**cannon:** a very large gun on wheels
[3]**microwave:** an electric cooker that uses waves of energy to cook or heat food
[4]**get (one's) hands on:** *(slang)* find; be able to use

Predict

Answer the questions. Then scan page 17 to check your answers.

1. One year, a team had an accident. What kind of accident did the team have?
2. In the accident, they 'took out a vendor'. What do the words 'vendor' and 'take out' mean?

One year, a team destroyed a vendor's table with their pumpkins!

One Punkin' Chunker' tells the story of an accident that happened at one of the contests. During the competition, his team tossed, or threw, their pumpkins backwards! 'We tossed two backwards last year. We actually **took out**[1] one of the **vendors'**[2] tables; there was a coffee table, and [we] just kind of destroyed it,' he says.

[1]**take out:** break; destroy
[2]**vendor:** seller of food, drinks, etc.

It's not just the pumpkins that can break. This year, Team Hypertension's pumpkin is very big and it breaks part of their machine. Luckily, despite this difficulty, their machine throws a pumpkin over 1,728 feet! Team Hypertension wins the contest again. After the event is over, John Huber happily announces, 'The King of Spring is still **in charge**!'[1]

The event is over for another year. But if you happen to be in Delaware at the right time, remember to look up at the sky. You just might have your own chance to see a real flying pumpkin!

---

[1]**in charge:** being the boss or leader

After You Read

1. A good heading for page 4 is:
A. Pumpkin-Rolling Contest.
B. Delaware's Interesting Contest.
C. People Like Pumpkins.
D. Confusing Contest Rules.

2. What is one of the rules of the contest?
A. No explosives.
B. Pumpkins must weigh ten pounds.
C. People must be serious.
D. People must not build machines.

3. The people who come to the contest are people:
A. who like to be inside.
B. who know nothing about machines.
C. who like to eat pumpkins.
D. from all over America.

4. According to page 9, the winner is the machine that throws the:
A. far.
B. farthest.
C. most far.
D. most furthest.

5. When do the teams start preparing for the contest?
A. October
B. September
C. September or October
D. November

6. How many people watch the contest?
A. over 20,000
B. 20,000
C. fewer than 20,000
D. more than 80,000

7. On page 10, the word 'strange' means:

A. terrible

B. unusual

C. boring

D. great

8. According to page 13, the most important part of the throwing machine is the:

A. size.

B. colour.

C. weight.

D. design.

9. On page 14, one team member uses a table as a practice item.

A. True

B. False

10. On page 17, what is the 'two' in 'we tossed two backwards'?

A. vendors' tables

B. coffee tables

C. pumpkins

D. kegs

11. Why is the King of Spring still in charge?

A. because his team won

B. because everybody knows him

C. because his machine broke

D. because his machine is the newest

12. What is the purpose of this story?

A. To show how far pumpkins can fly.

B. To introduce an unusual event.

C. To explain that catapulting is difficult.

D. To describe building a catapult.

CENTRAL HIGH NEWSPAPER

YEAR TEN PUPILS WIN CATAPULT

Every year the pupils of Central High School study European history, and every year there is one subject in which students are always very interested. They all love learning about the strange contraptions that ancient cultures used to fight their wars. One of the most interesting of these contraptions is the catapult. Long ago, invaders used this machine to throw huge rocks against the walls of castles. If the machine worked correctly, the rocks broke the wall. This allowed the fighters to enter the castle. These ancient catapults were usually heavy wooden contraptions.

Invaders Attacking an Ancient Castle with Catapults

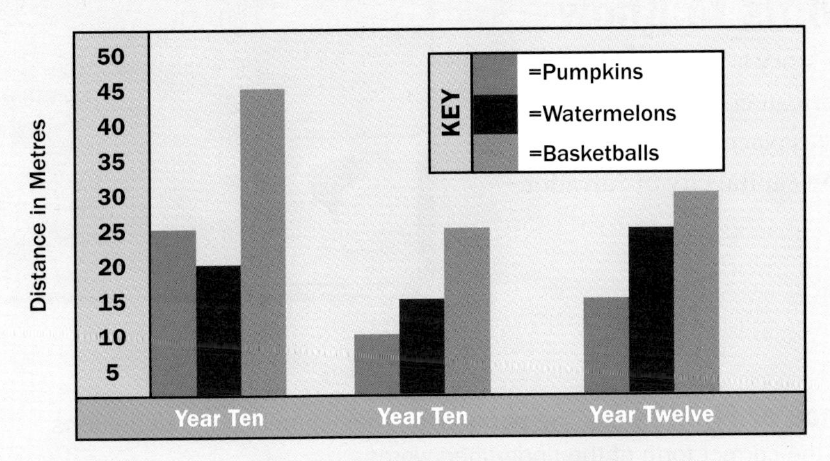

Catapult Competition Results 2008

Due to pupil interest in this ancient method of attack, the history department at Central High started the catapult competition ten years ago. Every year, teachers and pupils from the art, science, and history departments spend months planning and researching. Everyone works together and attempts to build catapults that work very well. Then, pupils in years ten, eleven, and twelve actually compete against each other to see who can throw the farthest. However, instead of throwing rocks, Central students throw pumpkins, watermelons, and basketballs. The team that throws these objects the farthest wins.

Everyone learns a lot from building the machines, and the competition itself is always very fun. Hundreds of friends and family members always attend.

This year, the year ten pupils surprised everyone by winning the competition. The results of the competition have been included in the graph above. As you can see, the year ten group did especially well with the basketball throwing. One reason that the year ten pupils may have won is because they studied the science of catapults carefully. They discovered that the arm of the catapult needs to be very long. They also realised that the machine has to be very heavy so that it stays still when it's used. Even though the year ten pupils had the least experience building catapults, they did an excellent job. Good work everybody!

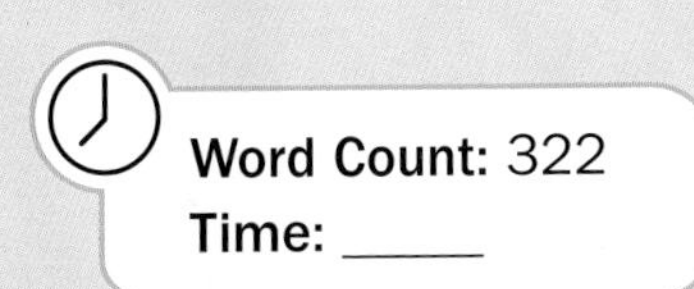

Words to Know

This story is set in the South American country of Brazil. It takes place in the state of Bahia, in the capital city of Salvador.

Dance or Fight? Read the paragraph. Then complete the definitions with the correct form of the underlined words.

This story is about a Brazilian martial art called *capoeira*. This unusual art form is really a combination of both dancing and fighting. In the 1800s, slaves in Brazil invented *capoeira* as a way of fighting against their owners and it later became a popular activity. Like most martial arts, practising *capoeira* brings together the body, mind, and soul. Also like martial arts, students of *capoeira* learn from a very experienced teacher, who is sometimes called a master.

1. A __________ is someone who is forced to work for no pay.
2. A __________ is a traditional skill of fighting that is done as a sport.
3. A __________ refers to a person who is very skilled in doing something.
4. A __________ is a mixture of two or more things.
5. The __________ is the part of a person that is not physical, which some people believe continues to exist after death.

B **Street Kids.** Read the definitions. Then complete the paragraph with the correct form of the words.

at risk: in a situation where something bad is likely to happen
beg: ask for food or money on the street
crime: an illegal activity
homeless: having no place to live
social worker: a person whose job is to help people who have problems because they are poor, old, or have difficulties with their family

In many countries of the world, there are street children and teens who are (1)__________ and must live without the care of parents or other adults. These kids often live in old, unused buildings, cars, parks, or on the street itself. Some have to (2)__________ for money with which to live. Others start committing (3)__________, such as stealing cars or money, to survive. Street kids are really (4)__________ for getting into difficult, dangerous situations. In this story, you will read about a group of (5)__________ who are trying to help the street kids of Salvador.

Practising *Capoeira*

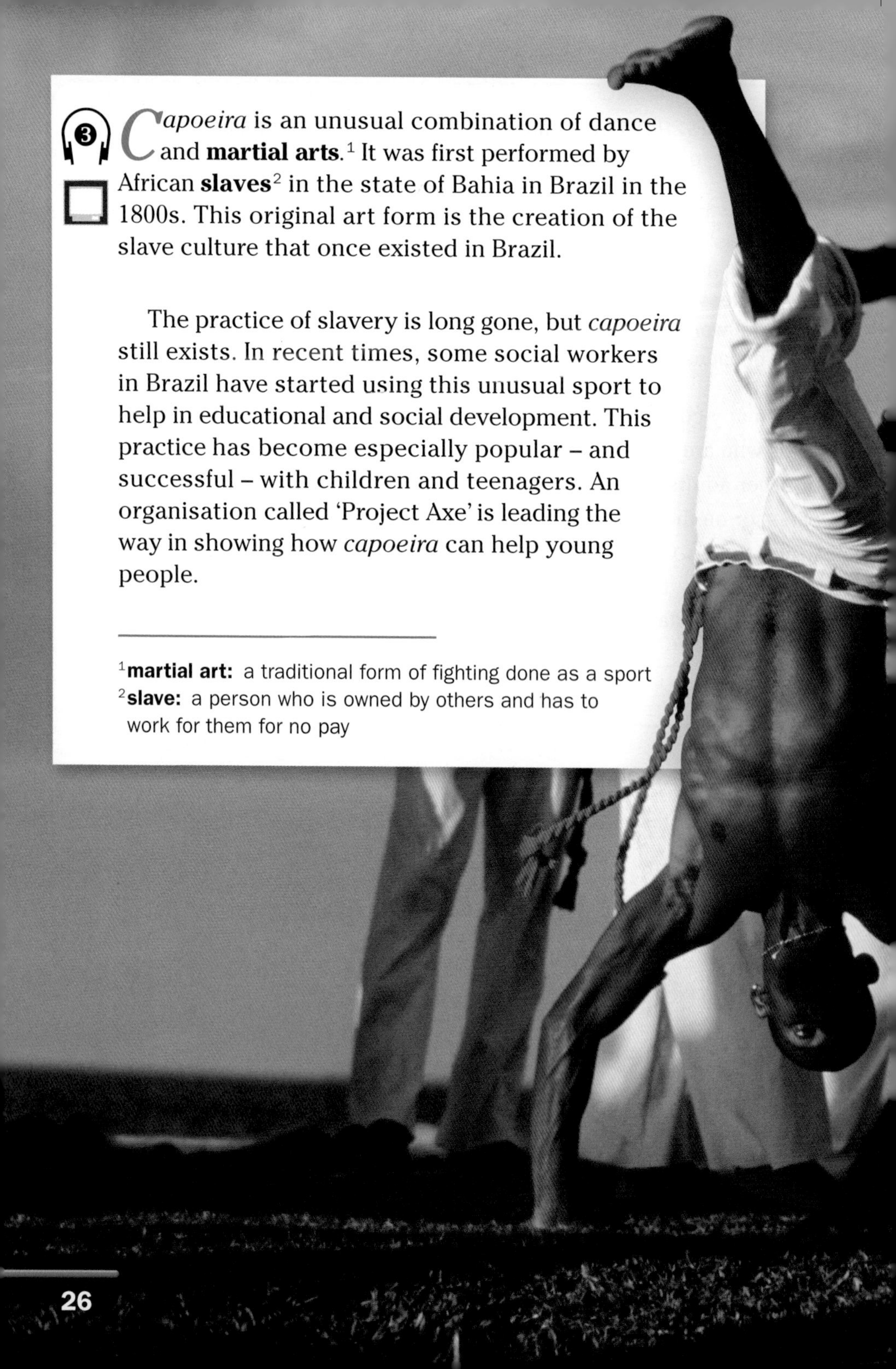

Capoeira is an unusual combination of dance and **martial arts**.[1] It was first performed by African **slaves**[2] in the state of Bahia in Brazil in the 1800s. This original art form is the creation of the slave culture that once existed in Brazil.

The practice of slavery is long gone, but *capoeira* still exists. In recent times, some social workers in Brazil have started using this unusual sport to help in educational and social development. This practice has become especially popular – and successful – with children and teenagers. An organisation called 'Project Axe' is leading the way in showing how *capoeira* can help young people.

---

[1]**martial art:** a traditional form of fighting done as a sport
[2]**slave:** a person who is owned by others and has to work for them for no pay

Skim for Gist

Read through the entire story quickly to answer the questions.

1. What is the story basically about?
2. What is the role of *capoeira* in helping the street kids?

PAULISTA
Amolador

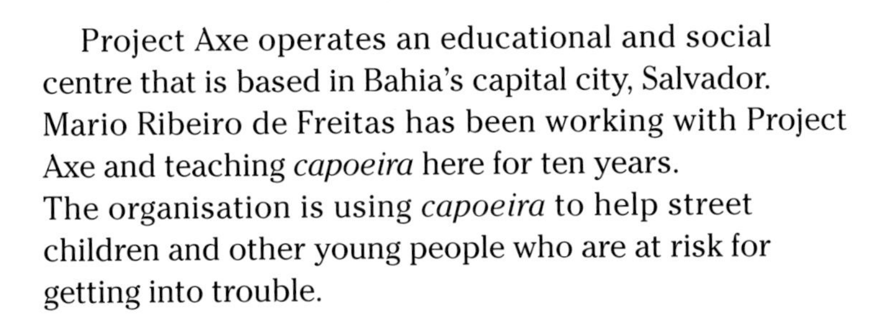

Project Axe operates an educational and social centre that is based in Bahia's capital city, Salvador. Mario Ribeiro de Freitas has been working with Project Axe and teaching *capoeira* here for ten years. The organisation is using *capoeira* to help street children and other young people who are at risk for getting into trouble.

Mario has practised *capoeira* for 25 years. He's now a master, which makes him a combination of teacher and **mentor**[1] for his students. While the activity does require physical strength, according to Mario, the martial art is about more than just keeping fit. It **integrates**[2] the strength of the body with the strength of the mind and soul. 'For these kids,' explains Mario, '*capoeira* is important not just for what it does for the body, but for what it does for the mind and soul.' It's clear that this *capoeira* master now really understands the power of this unusual fighting dance, but that wasn't always the case.

---

[1]**mentor:** an experienced person who gives help and advice to a less experienced person over a period of time

[2]**integrate:** bring two or more things together to become more effective

Years ago, Mario was just another young boy from a bad neighbourhood, but then *capoeira* helped him, he says. 'I studied with several *capoeira* masters and learned a **tremendous**[1] amount from them,' he explains. 'I took positive aspects from their lives and applied them to mine – not just to my teaching, but to my whole life, to my family,' he adds.

Project Axe's programmes are helping many of Salvador's children and teenagers who have run away from their homes. The **participants**[2] may be in trouble with the police or be in programmes which help people with drug problems. Axe workers make contact with many homeless kids out on the streets. Project Axe can help them, but first they have to make some changes.

---

[1]**tremendous:** very big; large
[2]**participant:** a person who takes part in an activity

Young people who are interested in joining one of Axe's several educational programmes must first agree to return to their own home or to go to a **foster home**.[1] Then, at the centre, students can focus on music, dance, or fashion design in addition to *capoeira*. They can also receive help with their basic education.

Another important aspect of the programme is that Project Axe works to make sure that the government knows about these kids. There are **considerable**[2] numbers of street kids in parts of Brazil, some of whom have 'disappeared' from official records. Confirming that they have governmental records is very important for the futures of these young people. If they don't have any records, they often can't get jobs or even go to school. In this way, Project Axe is also an essential part of helping these kids to really belong and function in society.

---

[1] **foster home:** a home in a social system taking care of children that cannot live in their own home
[2] **considerable:** large amount

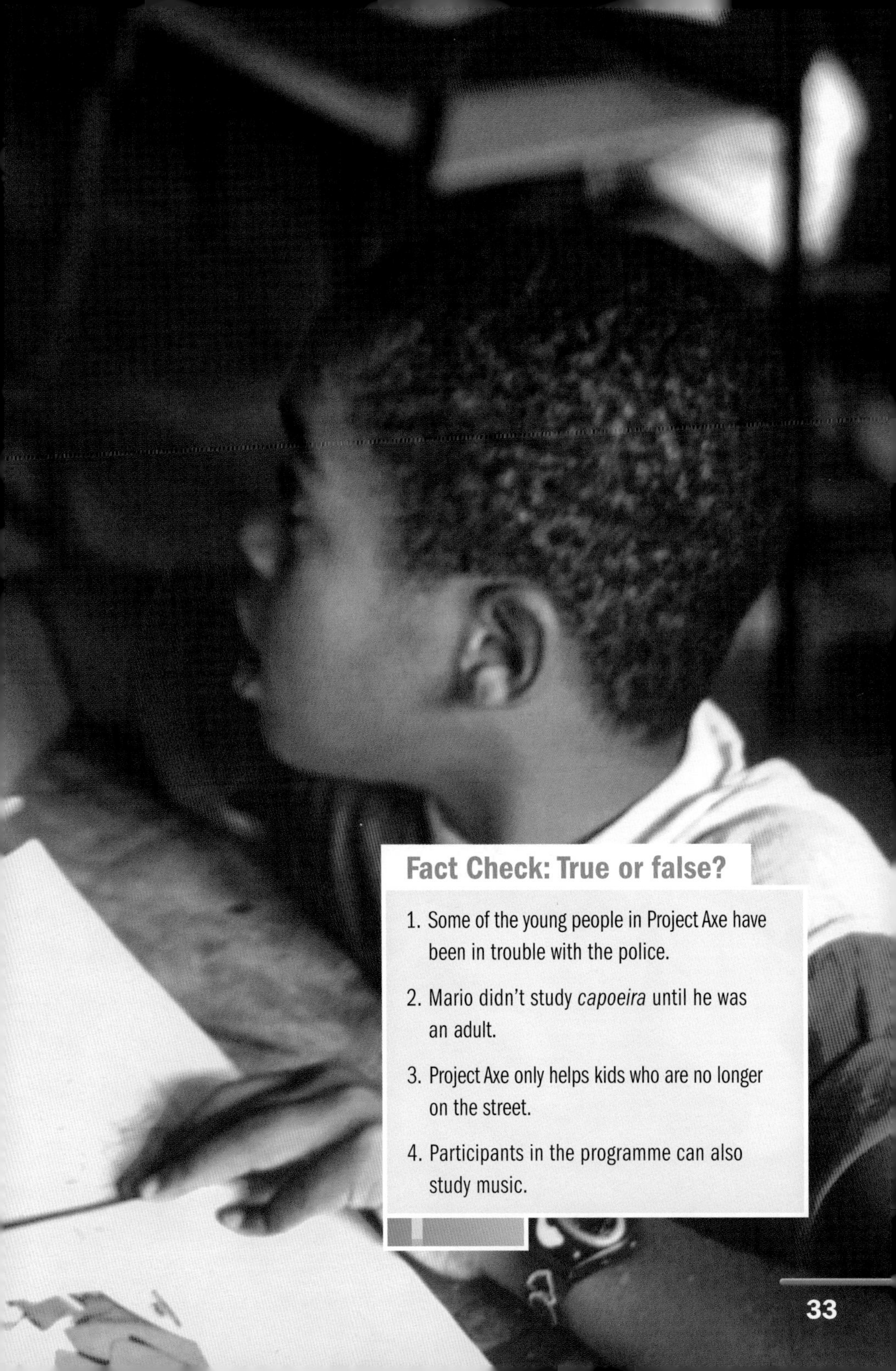

Fact Check: True or false?

1. Some of the young people in Project Axe have been in trouble with the police.
2. Mario didn't study *capoeira* until he was an adult.
3. Project Axe only helps kids who are no longer on the street.
4. Participants in the programme can also study music.

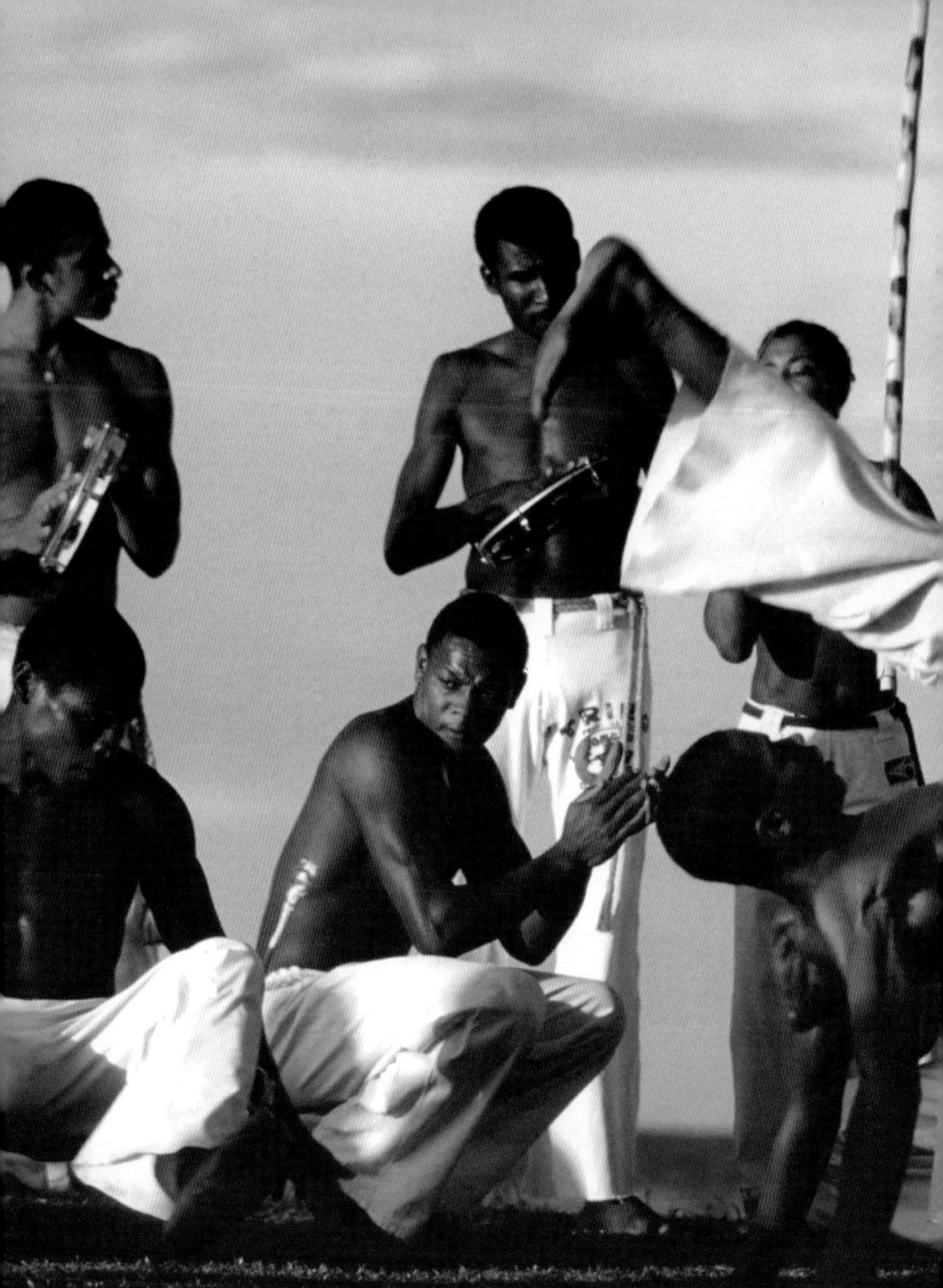

Mario says that *capoeira* also teaches the students to control their **behaviour**[1] and to treat others with respect. He says that this is most apparent when participants form a circle and perform *capoeira* as a group, which is also known as 'the circle'. He explains in his own words: 'Basically, I take what they have to offer – their body strength and their energy – and **mould**[2] it by integrating them into the group.' He then talks about how he does this, 'Once they are in the circle, which is the most **sacred**[3] moment of the *capoeira* process, I show them that there are **norms**,[4] rules and limits – within yourself and with others – that need to be followed.'

---

[1]**behaviour:** the way sb acts or speaks
[2]**mould:** form into a shape
[3]**sacred:** held in high respect for religious or other reasons
[4]**norm:** rule; standard way of behaving

Capoeira has a long and interesting history. Hundreds of years ago, slaves in Brazil first practised it as a way of opposing their owners. However, they made the fighting actions look like a dance so that their owners would not know what they were doing.

After slavery was **abolished**[1] in Brazil in 1888, *capoeira* became popular as both **amusement**[2] and sport. It also helped to raise the ex-slaves' awareness of themselves as Afro-Brazilians, or Brazilians with African **heritage**.[3]

---

[1] **abolish:** stop; make illegal
[2] **amusement:** an enjoyable way of spending your time
[3] **heritage:** beliefs, traditions, history, etc. passed from parents to their children

Today, *capoeira* is helping street kids **give up**[1] **drugs**[2] and crime and create new lives for themselves. Fifteen-year-old Milton Dos Santos is a real-life example of how *capoeira* has helped homeless teenagers. 'My situation has totally changed. I was living on the street. I was homeless. I did a lot of drugs and I was involved in selling stolen cars,' says Milton. 'Axe got me off the streets,' he explains, 'I'm studying *capoeira* and I don't do that other stuff anymore,' he continues, 'and I have an excellent master. My life is better.'

For these kids, another important part of *capoeira* is respect. 'I was on the street, begging for money,' says another 15-year-old boy, 'then I heard about Axe and they offered me a place. I love *capoeira*, especially the circle, with two people giving respect and getting respect. We perform and learn to respect each other.'

---

[1]**give up:** to stop doing or having sth
[2]**drug:** an illegal substance that affects the body and mind

In Mario's classroom at Project Axe, his students may still be a little nervous and a little unsure about their future, but there are signs of progress in their lives. One of his *capoeira* classes is now preparing for a two-week trip to Italy. They're going to perform for audiences there. It will be a long journey, but these young people have already come a long way. They've made it from the streets of Salvador to a safer, healthier place. The martial art of *capoeira* has given these young people hope for a better future.

After You Read

1. Who created *capoeira*?
A. street children
B. social workers
C. Brazilians in Africa
D. slaves

2. Mario Riberio de Freitas has worked ________ Project Axe ________ years.
A. with, in
B. on, for
C. for, during
D. at, of

3. What does Mario think is the most important benefit of *capoeira*?
A. strengthening the mind and soul
B. learning protection
C. developing physical power
D. building a strong body

4. On page 30, when Mario says 'applied them', what does 'them' refer to?
A. *capoeira* masters
B. his family
C. *capoeira* steps
D. positive aspects

5. Street children who want to participate in Project Axe must first:
A. go to Salvador.
B. talk to Mario.
C. find somewhere to live.
D. fix a drug problem.

6. The word 'basic' on page 32 can be replaced by:
A. introductory
B. essential
C. planned
D. popularized

7. Brazilians need government records to:
A. get a job.
B. find a foster home.
C. have children.
D. participate in Project Axe.

8. Why does the writer give details about the *capoeira* circle?
A. to show that *capeoira* is a religion
B. to show that Mario is the master
C. to show that *capeoira* teaches social behaviour
D. to explain that rules must be followed

9. What's the meaning of the word 'awareness' on page 36?
A. society
B. identity
C. contentment
D. knowledge

10. Which of the following is a suitable heading for page 36?
A. A Modern Dance
B. Secret Protection
C. Entertainment Only
D. Dancing to Freedom

11. What's the main purpose of the views expressed on page 39?
A. to describe lives improved by *capoeira*
B. to explain why children love to perform *capoeira*
C. to show the hard life that street children have
D. to teach us about crime in Salvador

12. Mario's teenagers have come a long way ________ their fight for a better life.
A. to
B. by
C. in
D. on

www.sport*blog.sa

CAPOEIRA CLUB

Capoeira Q and A

HOW CAN I FIND A *CAPOEIRA* SCHOOL?

POSTED: Peter on Sat Aug 9 @ 2:00 pm: I have checked several martial arts websites and I can't find a *capoeira* school in my area.

RE: HOW CAN I FIND A *CAPOEIRA* SCHOOL?

POSTED: Lionel on Sat Aug 9 @ 9:13 pm: Go to the home page for this website. In the upper left corner, you will find a place to search for schools by city, county or country. If you still can't find anything in your area, don't worry! We get lists of several new schools every day.

I WANT TO IMPROVE

POSTED: Daniel on Mon Aug 4 @ 5:01 pm: I've been practising *capoeira* for about six months. I have learnt a tremendous amount, but I want to get even better. It seems to take a long time to learn everything. Does anybody have any ideas for how I can improve quickly?

***Capoeira* Class at My School**

Fast Facts about *Capoeira*

- The countries with the most *capoeira* schools are Brazil (about 300) and the U.S. (over 500).
- In *capoeira*, a circle of people, called a *roda*, watch as two players compete in a fight-like dance called a *jugo*, or game.
- Music is an important part of *capoeira*. It sets the style and speed of the game.
- When a student is accepted into a *capoeira* group, he or she is given a belt (*corda*) and a special name (*apelido*).

RE: I WANT TO IMPROVE

POSTED: Marcia on Mon Aug 4 @ 7:44 pm: It takes time for your body to learn the movements and get strong. And it takes time for your mind to integrate what it needs to learn as well. However, here are some things that might help. Even though it may seem boring, find a mentor to help you practise the basics over and over again. Go to the gym and lift weights to help you get strong fast. You can also watch videos to learn new combinations of movements. Good luck!

WOMEN IN *CAPOEIRA*

POSTED: Maria on Mon Aug 4 @ 5:20 pm: I have discovered that if I hit a man while fighting, people think it's because he wasn't looking or he needs to improve his skills. But if I hit a woman, they think that it's just because she's a woman and they think I shouldn't have hit her. That really bothers me! Can't I treat men and women equally?

RE: WOMEN IN *CAPOEIRA*

POSTED: Ramon on Tue Aug 5 @ 1:00 am: Yes, you're right. It's not a fair way to look at things. A woman can kick and hit just as hard as a man, and they can avoid being hit just as well. Some women are better than men at *capoeira* and some men are better than women. We should assess the abilities of each person we fight individually.

Words to Know

This story is set in England, in the United Kingdom. It happens in the town of Brockworth.

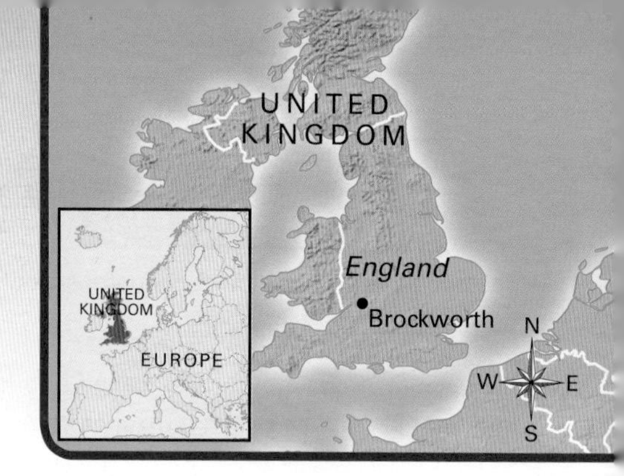

A At the Races. Here are some words you will see in the story. Complete the definitions with words in the box.

cheer	prize	route
crowd	race	spectators

1. The road or way you follow to get from one place to another place is a __________.
2. An event in which people try to be the fastest to do something is a __________.
3. To shout loudly to encourage someone is to __________.
4. A large group of people is a __________.
5. __________ are the people who are watching a sporting event, show, etc.
6. A __________ is something that is given to someone who wins a competition.

B Cheese-Rolling Races. Read the paragraph and look at the picture. Then match each word to the correct definition.

In England, many towns have traditional competitions. In them, competitors usually try to win a game or contest. However, the annual cheese-rolling race in Brockworth is a little unusual. At the start of the race, someone rolls a wheel of cheese down a very steep hill. Then, the competitors run after the cheese. The first person to reach the bottom of the hill is the winner.

1. competition _____	**a.** rising or falling sharply
2. competitor _____	**b.** move in one direction by turning over and over
3. annual _____	**c.** person who takes part in a race or contest
4. roll _____	**d.** once every year
5. wheel of cheese _____	**e.** a large, round piece of cheese
6. steep _____	**f.** an organised event in which people try to be the best or fastest

The Annual Cheese-Rolling Race

Cheese-rolling has been a tradition in the town of Brockworth since the early 1800s. But what happens in this old and locally famous competition? It's quite simple, really. First, the competitors come together at the top of a hill named 'Cooper's Hill'. The **slope**[1] of the hill is very steep – almost 45 degrees! And after that? They wait, but wait for what?

[1]**slope:** the side of a hill or mountain

FFICIAL
Cooper's Hill has
a very steep slope!

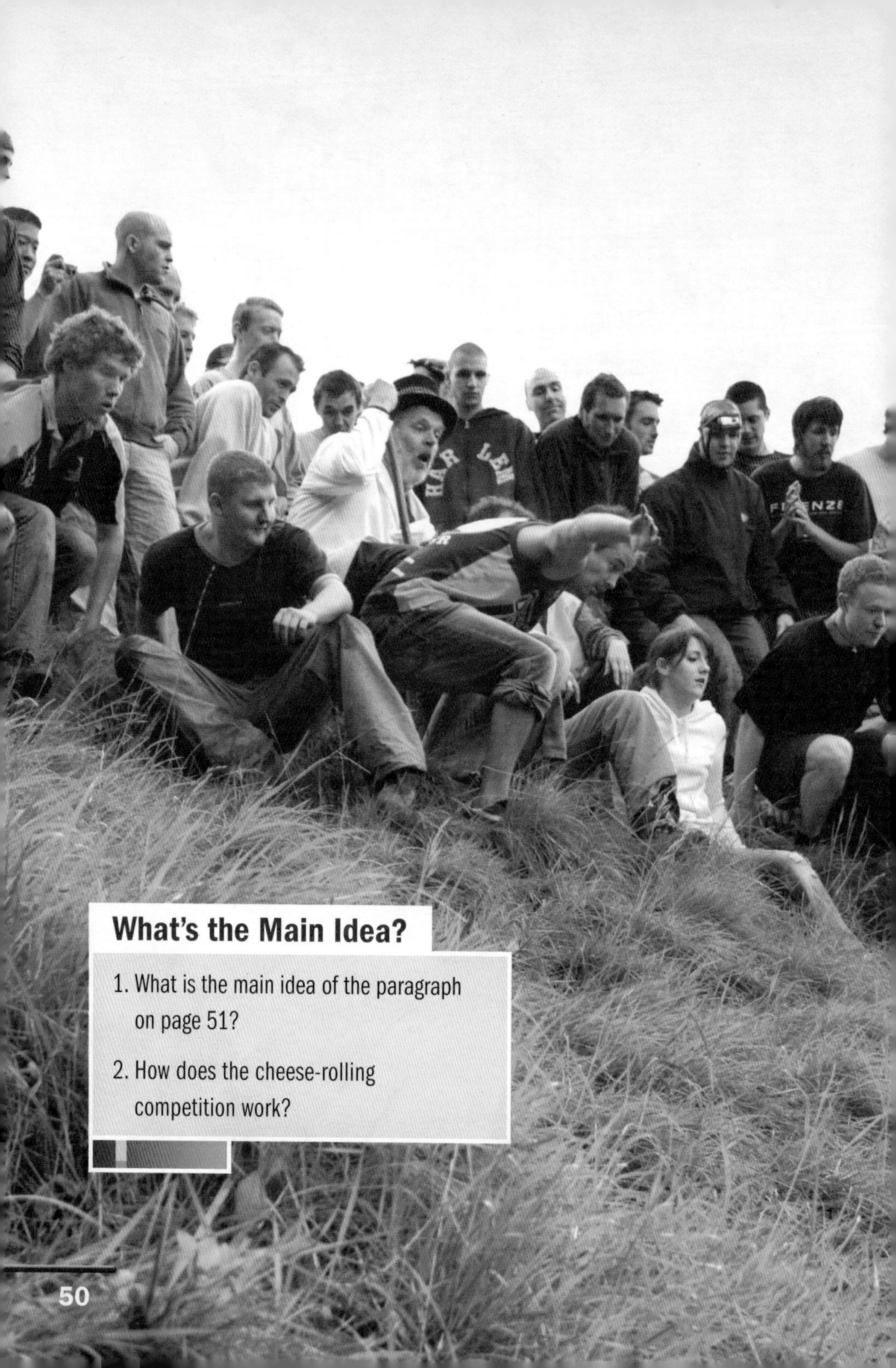

What's the Main Idea?

1. What is the main idea of the paragraph on page 51?
2. How does the cheese-rolling competition work?

They wait for someone to push a very large wheel of cheese down the hill. The competitors then **run** very quickly **after**[1] it. The cheese may reach up to 40 miles per hour. The competitors go quite fast too. The first one to the bottom of the hill wins. What's the prize for such an unusual event? It's the wheel of cheese – of course!

---

[1] **run after:** to chase sb or sth

The first winner of the day in this year's competition is Craig Brown, a **pub**[1] worker. He's happy to be the winner, but he's also very tired. What did he do to win the race? Craig says that his plan was simple; the most important thing is just to continue running. 'Keep [on] going,' he says, 'and try to get your **balance**[2] back.' He then adds, 'It's steeper than you could ever think. You'd have to run down there to really believe how steep it is!'

---

[1]**pub:** place where drinks and food are served
[2]**balance:** ability to stand up and not fall over due to unequal weight

Many people enjoy the cheese-rolling races of Brockworth. However, the race can be dangerous. You never know the route the cheese will take as it rolls down the hill. A few years ago, 30 people were **injured**[1] in an **accident**[2] at a race. One of the cheeses rolled down the hill too quickly and suddenly went into the crowd. Some of the spectators were hit by the cheese. Now, the competition route has **crash barriers.**[3] They protect the crowd from the cheese – and from the competitors!

---

[1]**injure:** to hurt a person or an animal
[2]**accident:** a bad thing which happens unexpectedly
[3]**crash barrier:** short wall along a competition route to protect spectators

Crash barriers protect the spectators at the races.

SECURITY

It's not just the spectators who get injured, the competitors do as well. This is especially true when the weather is very cold. There are also more injuries when there hasn't been much rain before the race. One organiser for the event explains, 'It's when the ground is really hard … that's when the injuries are going to happen.'

But the hard ground doesn't seem to stop the competitors. Every year there are a lot of people who follow Craig Brown's suggestion; they just 'keep on going' down Cooper's Hill. But what about Craig? How did he do in the remaining cheese-rolling races?

Well, Craig's plan to just 'keep on going' **unfortunately**[1] failed. When he tried to keep on going in the second race, he lost his balance and fell – again and again! At the time, he was trying to get the competition's version of a 'double'. He wanted to win two cheese wheels in one day. But instead of going home with a 'double cheese,' Craig went home with only one cheese, and maybe a few **bruises**![2]

---

[1]**unfortunately:** unluckily
[2]**bruise:** a dark purple or black mark on the skin from an injury

So, what **drives**[1] these runners? What makes them do it? Are they **crazy**?[2] One cheese runner thinks they may be. 'It is dangerous,' he says as he looks at the very steep slope of Cooper's Hill. 'If I'm running down [the hill], [I] must be crazy. Yeah, I must be crazy …' he decides with a smile.

---

[1]**drive:** to force sb to do sth
[2]**crazy:** mad; not sensible

The cheese racers of Brockworth may just be crazy. However, the crowds keep on cheering, and the competitors keep on running – year after year. It seems that a lot of people are very happy to try this dangerous run. Is it for the **fame**?[1] Is it for the fun? We may never know, but you can almost be sure of one thing; it's not only for the prize. It's more than just cheese that makes people want to win Brockworth's annual cheese-rolling race!

[1]**fame:** being known for one's achievements or skills

What do you think?

1. Do you think the cheese runners are crazy?
2. Would you like to be a competitor in this cheese-rolling competition? Why or why not?
3. Do you participate in any activities which other people might think are 'crazy'?

After You Read

1. On page 48, what does 'locally' mean?
A. traditional
B. in the area
C. ancient
D. totally

2. How long has this competition been happening?
A. forty-five years
B. less than two hundred years
C. over two hundred years
D. not in text

3. The goal of the competition is:
A. to finish first.
B. to follow the competitors.
C. to be quicker than the cheese.
D. to roll cheese down a hill.

4. On page 51, 'it' in 'quickly after it' refers to a:
A. competitor
B. prize
C. person
D. wheel of cheese

5. Choose the best heading for page 52.
A. Tired But Happy Loser
B. Hill Is Not So Bad
C. Pub Worker Gets Cheese
D. Balance Is Unimportant

6. On page 52, how does Craig Brown describe the competition?
A. really good fun
B. not at all tiring
C. harder than it looks
D. easy if you don't stop

7. On page 56, 'they' in 'they just "keep on going"' refers to the:
A. competitors
B. race organisers
C. spectators
D. none of the above

8. Once the cheese crashed __________ a crowd of spectators.
A. on
B. under
C. with
D. into

9. Cold, dry weather makes the race safer.
A. True
B. False

10. What happens to Craig Brown in the second race?
A. He loses his balance.
B. He gets a double.
C. He wins the cheese.
D. He is badly injured.

11. What's the purpose of page 60?
A. To prove that the competition is safe.
B. To show the competitors are unhappy.
C. To show that the runners are crazy.
D. none of the above

12. What does the writer probably think about the competition?
A. The spectators cheer too much.
B. The race is too dangerous.
C. The competitors like the fame and fun.
D. The prize is very good cheese.

BED RACING

It Isn't Crazy After All

Bed racing is becoming more popular in certain areas of the U.S. A bed race is a competition where teams of people push beds along a specific route. The route often goes through the middle of a city or town. The competing teams attempt to roll their beds along the route faster than anyone else. However, these are not just any beds. Racing beds often have very big wheels and the competitors sometimes paint them in some very interesting ways.

Most bed races are about having fun and raising money for the community.

2007 Race Results

	1st Place	2nd Place	3rd Place	Last Place
Team	*Sleepwalkers*	*Morning Suns*	*Fast Times*	*Sleeping Beauties*
Time	4 minutes, 31 seconds	4 minutes, 42 seconds	5 minutes, 10 seconds	14 minutes, 14 seconds

The teams build their own beds and practise for weeks before the race. However, race organisers often have firm rules about building and racing beds. For example: the beds must be a certain size, they can't have an engine, and they must have four wheels. In addition, there must be no more than six people pushing the bed and only one person can sit in the bed.

As long as the teams follow the rules, they can use their imaginations for everything else. Some beds are covered with flowers. Other beds look like crazy boats. To add to the fun, people often wear strange and unusual clothing.

On race days, large crowds of spectators come to cheer for their favourite team. These members of the community usually give money to their favourite team. However, the money doesn't go to the team members. It goes to organisations that help people in need. In the past, bed races have raised lots of money to provide health care for children and to help homeless people. At the end of the race, teams are often listed in a table like the one above. Most of these teams don't even get a prize for winning. These bed races are obviously not serious events. The important thing is to raise money for the community and to have fun.

Word Count: 312
Time: _____

Grammar Focus: Intensive Pronouns: Singular

- Intensive pronouns are used to emphasise a noun or pronoun.
- Singular intensive pronouns end in '-*self*'.
- Intensive pronouns have a different function than reflexive pronouns, which are usually the objects of verbs or prepositions in clauses, where the subject and object are the same person or thing, for example:

  The girl hurt herself when she slipped on the icy steps.
  Everyone learns a lot (…), and the competition itself is always very fun.
  You can go if you want to, but I myself am staying here.
  She herself must decide what she needs to do.
  The prime minister delivered the good news himself.
  You yourself said that the principal wants to see her.

Grammar Practice: Intensive Pronouns: Singular

A. Fill in the blanks with the correct singular intensive pronoun.

e.g. I ___*myself*___ don't have a garden, but my friends do.

1. The machine was fine, but the pumpkin __________ was too big to throw.
2. You can't expect other people to like the book if you __________ don't like it.
3. I can't tell you what he plans to do because he __________ doesn't know.
4. I hear that the princess __________ will present the award.

Grammar Focus: Intensive Pronouns: Plural

- Plural intensive pronouns end in '-*selves*'.

  The teams themselves decide what kind of machine to build.
  You yourselves are responsible for how much you learn.
  We can make a decision on the matter ourselves. We don't need to wait for the boss.

Grammar Practice: Intensive Pronouns: Plural

B. Fill in the blanks with the correct plural intensive pronoun.

e.g. My brothers and I built the machine ___*ourselves*___.

1. The students at Jones School elected the class president __________ .

2. Well done, class! Give __________ a round of applause!

3. We __________ are going to the contest, but you don't have to go.

4. The residents __________ helped each other escape from the burning building.

Grammar Focus: Relative Pronouns as Subjects and Objects

Relative Pronouns as Subjects

- When used as subjects, relative pronouns are followed by a verb:
  The tall dancer is handsome. He is in the show.
  The tall dancer, who is in the show, is handsome.

Relative Pronouns as Objects

- When used as objects, relative pronouns are followed by subjects, usually nouns or pronouns:
  She asked new players to join the team. The new players were strong.
  The new players, who(m) she asked to join the team, were strong.

- Relative pronouns introduce relative clauses that can be subjects or objects of the clause. Use *which* or *that* for things and *who*, *whom* or *that* for people.

- All relative pronouns can be used as both subjects and objects except for *whom*. *Whom* is always an object and is considered somewhat formal. *Who* is often used as the object form in American English.

Grammar Practice: Relative Pronouns as Subjects and Objects

Rewrite the sentences so that each of them contains a relative pronoun.

e.g. Project Axe is a programme in Brazil. Project Axe is a programme that helps street children.
Project Axe, which is a programme in Brazil, helps street children.

1. The *capoeira* master is also a mentor. The *capoeira* master is respected by many.

____

2. That martial art is called *capoeira*. It is also a kind of dance.

____

3. Mary knows those students. They go to her school.

____

Grammar Focus: Phrasal Verbs

- A phrasal verb consists of a verb + preposition. Often the meaning is idiomatic.
  put + on = get dressed　　　　*put + off = postpone*

- Some phrasal verbs take objects.
  I put on my coat.

- With some phrasal verbs, the object can be placed before the preposition. These verbs are called **separable** phrasal verbs.
  I put on my coat. = I put my coat on.

- With other phrasal verbs, the object cannot be placed before the preposition. These verbs are called **inseparable** phrasal verbs.
  They ran after the ball. NOT *They ran the ball after.*

Separable phrasal verbs

fill	out	take	off
get	back	turn	on
put	on	turn	off
put	out	throw	away

Inseparable phrasal verbs

run	after
fall	down

Grammar Practice: Phrasal verbs

Complete each of the sentences with one of the phrasal verbs in the following box.

keep on	~~get back~~	put on	run after	turn off	fill out

e.g. I had a cold all last week. I hope I *get back* my energy soon.

1. It's very cold today. Be sure to ___________ your jacket when you go out.
2. Don't stop now! If you ___________ exercising every day, you'll get stronger and feel better.
3. If you want to enter the Cheese-Rolling Race, you must ___________ this form.
4. I sometimes forget to ___________ my computer when I go to bed. That wastes a lot of energy.
5. In Brockworth, people ___________ a big cheese as it rolls down a hill.

Video Practice

A. Watch the video of *Flying Pumpkins!* and circle the word you hear.

1. 'Every year in the state of Delaware, a group of people have an interesting (contest/competition) ...'
2. 'The rules are simple. The (kegs/pumpkins) must weigh at least eight pounds ...'
3. 'Some take it very seriously, some (won't/don't) ...'
4. 'We started out with a little contraption with about (40/14) garage door springs on it.'
5. 'The machine that throws – or "chunks" – a pumpkin the (farthest/best) wins.'

B. Watch the video again and write down the word or words you hear.

1. 'The contest began with only three __________ and a few friends to watch.'
2. 'But people do have to think about the design of __________ if they want to win.'
3. 'Now, Punkin' Chunkin' machines can be anything from a catapult to __________.'
4. 'We chunk pumpkins, watermelons, kegs, toilets, __________, microwaves, tyres ...'
5. 'This year, Team Hypertension's pumpkin is very big and it __________ part of their machine.'

Video Practice

C. Watch the video of *Capoeira: The Fighting Dance* and write the vocabulary word or phrase you hear.

1. 'This is *capoeira* – an unusual ____________ of dance and martial arts.'
2. 'It was first performed by African ____________ in Bahia, Brazil, in the 1800s.'
3. 'The organisation uses *capoeira* to help street kids and others who are ____________.'
4. 'Axe workers make contact with many ____________ kids out on the streets.'

D. Watch the video again and circle the preposition you hear.

1. '… I show them that there are norms, rules, and limits, (in/within) yourself, and with others, that need to be followed.'
2. 'It also helped to raise ex-slaves' awareness (of/about) themselves as Afro-Brazilians.'
3. 'My situation has totally changed. I was living (of/on) the street.'
4. 'It'll be a long journey, but they've already come a long way. They've made it (from/on) the streets of Salvador to a safer, healthier place!'

Video Practice

E. Watch the video of *Cheese-Rolling Races* and circle the word you hear.

1. 'Then, someone (pushes/rolls) a very large wheel of cheese down the steep slope.'
2. 'Many people (like/enjoy) the cheese-rolling races, however they can be dangerous.'
3. 'One of the cheeses (went/rolled) down the hill too quickly and unexpectedly went into the crowd.'
4. 'Now, the competition route has crash barriers to protect the (people/crowd).'
5. 'Craig's plan to just "keep on going" unfortunately (didn't work/ failed) in this second race.'
6. 'So, what drives these runners? Are they crazy? One cheese runner (thinks/says) they may be.'

F. Watch the video again and fill in the word you hear.

1. 'Cheese-rolling has been a tradition in the town of Brockworth since the early ___________.'
2. 'The cheese may reach up to ___________ miles per hour ...'
3. 'The ___________ winner of the day is Craig Brown, a pub worker.'
4. 'A few years ago, ___________ people were injured in an accident at a race.'
5. '... he was trying to get the competition's version of a "double play", winning ___________ cheese wheels in one day.'

Exit Test: Flying Pumpkins!

(1) One of the teams that competes in the pumpkin throwing competition every year is called 'Team Hypertension'. **(2)** They think that they have the very best pumpkin-throwing machine. **(3)** John Huber, a member of Team Hypertension, says that their catapult is well engineered. **(4)** It uses a set of garage door springs to throw the pumpkin very far. **(5)** It is important to remember that a good machine isn't enough. **(6)** Winning teams spend a lot of time practising. **(7)** They sometimes practise throwing some rather strange objects, including watermelons, refrigerators, and even microwaves. **(8)** Sometimes, however, things don't go well. **(9)** One year a team threw their pumpkins backwards. **(10)** That caused one of them to hit a coffee table and destroy it. **(11)** This year Team Hypertension won the contest. **(12)** Their catapult broke during the competition, but they still won!

A. Read the paragraph and answer the questions.

1. Team members are probably _______ most of the time.
A. worried
B. relaxed
C. confident
D. serious

2. Why did the pumpkin hit the coffee table and destroy it?
A. The machine broke.
B. The coffee table was too close to the machine.
C. The machine was not well engineered.
D. The team threw their pumpkins backwards.

3. Where should this sentence go? Many start practising weeks before the contest.
A. after sentence 2
B. after sentence 6
C. after sentence 9
D. after sentence 10

4. The best heading for this paragraph is _______.
A. How to Make a Good Catapult
B. Throwing Strange Things
C. A Winning Team
D. When a Machine Breaks

5. The team members _______ built the catapult.
A. itself
B. themselves
C. yourselves
D. himself

6. John Huber _______ says that the catapult is well engineered.
A. myself
B. itself
C. himself
D. themselves

7. A machine that keeps things cold is a _______.
A. keg
B. cannon
C. refrigerator
D. bucket

8. The word 'them' in sentence 10 refers to _______.

B. Read the sentences. Write 'True' or 'False'. Refer to the paragraph if necessary.

9. Team Hypertension thinks that their machine needs more springs.
____

10. A machine used to throw things is called a catapult. _______

EXIT TEST: *CAPOEIRA*: THE FIGHTING DANCE

(1) Mario Ribeiro de Frietas is a social worker who has practised *capoeira* for 25 years. **(2)** He began his life in a bad neighborhood in Bahia, Brazil. **(3)** Luckily he discovered *capoeira* when he was quite young and it changed his life completely. **(4)** Mario studied with several different masters and learned a lot from them. **(5)** Later, he went to work for an organisation called 'Project Axe' in Salvador, the capital of Bahia. **(6)** This organisation provides educational and social programmes for homeless street children in Bahia. **(7)** However, before young people can join the group, they must return to their original family or find a foster family, or replacement family, to live with. **(8)** Mario has taught *capoeira* at Project Axe for the past ten years. **(9)** Now he has become a master. **(10)** He says that this martial art helps increase fitness. **(11)** However, he explains, it is also valuable because it strengthens the mind and the soul. **(12)** It teaches children to control their behaviour and to respect other people.

A. Read the paragraph and answer the questions.

11. Salvador is ______.
A. the capital of Brazil
B. the name of an organisation
C. the capital of Bahia
D. the name of a martial art

12. The word 'it' in sentence 11 refers to ______.
A. fitness
B. a foster family
C. Project Axe
D. *capoeira*

13. Today Mario probably lives ______.
A. in a bad neighbourhood
B. with a group of *capoeira* masters
C. in the capital of Brazil
D. in Salvador

14. The purpose of this paragraph is ______.
A. to show how *capoeira* changed Mario's life
B. to describe the problems of homeless people in Bahia
C. to explain why Mario started practising *capoeira*
D. to describe the work of Project Axe

15. Where should this sentence go?
He took positive aspects of their lives and applied them to his.
A. after sentence 2
B. after sentence 4
C. after sentence 7
D. after sentence 10

16. Which of the following does not happen to young people who practise *capoeira*?
A. They become more fit.
B. They get jobs right away.
C. They respect other people more.
D. They learn to control their behaviour.

B. Answer the questions.

17. If homeless people need help, they should call a ______.
A. slave
B. social worker
C. martial art
D. combination

18. Another word for illegal activity is ______.
A. crime
B. soul
C. master
D. beg

19. Several people were sitting in the chairs, ______ had been placed in neat rows.
A. whom
B. who
C. which
D. what

20. Which of the underlined words is incorrect?
The social worker, which was visiting Brazil, wanted to learn more about *Capoeira*.
A. which
B. visiting
C. wanted
D. about

Exit Test: Cheese-Rolling Races

(1) The cheese races held at Brockworth, England, each year are a lot of fun. **(2)** At these races, someone pushes a very large cheese down a steep hill and runners run after it. **(3)** The competitors really want to win one of the cheeses. **(4)** The hill where the races are held is very steep, but runners don't seem to mind. **(5)** It just makes them go faster. **(6)** Both spectators and runners seem to be having a good time. **(7)** Everyone is laughing and smiling. **(8)** Some people say the runners are crazy, and I must say I agree. **(9)** The crowd cheers, 'Go! Go! Go!' and this makes the runners go even faster. **(10)** They sometimes run so fast that they fall and get hurt. **(11)** In fact five years ago, 30 spectators were injured when a cheese rolled into the crowd. **(12)** But that didn't stop people from coming back the next year. **(13)** The races are just too much fun!

A. Read the paragraph and answer the questions.

21. What is the main idea of this paragraph?
A. The cheese races are dangerous.
B. The competitors run very fast.
C. The cheese races are a lot of fun.
D. The runners are crazy.

22. Because the crowd shouts, 'Go! Go! Go!', ______.
A. the runners go faster
B. the spectators start running too
C. people cover their ears
D. some runners get hurt

23. The writer thinks that ______.
A. the spectators are crazy
B. the races should be stopped
C. the runners are crazy
D. the spectators should not cheer for the runners

24. How many spectators were injured watching the race a few years ago?
A. five
B. twelve
C. ten
D. thirty

25. The Brockworth cheese races are held ______.
A. in the winter
B. every year
C. in the rain
D. every five years

26. Where should this sentence go?
I would never run in one of these races.
A. after sentence 3
B. after sentence 7
C. after sentence 8
D. after sentence 12

B. Answer the questions.

27. A large group of people is called a ______.
A. crowd
B. competition
C. prize
D. route

28. A person who watches a sporting event is a ______.
A. competitor
B. spectator
C. racer
D. cheer

29. The racer fell over but he stood up and kept ______ running.
A. at
B. in
C. up
D. on

30. Sometimes it's hard to ______ your balance back when you start to fall.
A. get
B. take
C. find
D. give

Key 答案

Flying Pumpkins!

Words to Know: A. 1. refrigerator **2.** catapult **3.** pumpkins **4.** kegs **5.** cannon **6.** garage door springs **7.** watermelons **8.** bucket **B. 1.** 3.6 **2.** 119.97 **3.** 535.68

Fact Check: 1. Delaware **2.** the Punkin' Chunkin' Contest **3.** to throw a pumpkin the farthest with a machine **4.** over 20 years ago

Predict: 1. One team threw two pumpkins backwards.
2. A 'vendor' sells food, drinks, etc. and 'take out' means to break or destroy.

After You Read: 1. B **2.** A **3.** D **4.** B **5.** C **6.** A **7.** B **8.** D **9.** B **10.** C **11.** A **12.** B

Capoeira: The Fighter Dance

Words to Know: A. 1. slave **2.** martial art **3.** master **4.** combination **5.** soul **B. 1.** homeless **2.** beg **3.** crimes **4.** at risk **5.** social workers

Skim for Gist: (suggested answers) **1.** The story is about how Project Axe helps poor street kids in Brazil through *capoeira*. **2.** *Capoeira* teaches the kids how to control their behaviour and to respect others. It integrates their bodies, minds, and souls, and gives them hope for a better future.

Fact Check: 1. True **2.** False **3.** True **4.** True

After You Read: 1. D **2.** B **3.** A **4.** D **5.** C **6.** A **7.** A **8.** C **9.** D **10.** D **11.** A **12.** C

Cheese-Rolling Races

Words to Know: A. 1. route **2.** race **3.** cheer **4.** crowd **5.** Spectators **6.** prize **B. 1.** f **2.** c **3.** d **4.** b **5.** e **6.** a

What's the Main Idea: (suggested answers) **1.** It describes how the cheese-rolling competition works. **2.** Participants push a wheel of cheese down a hill and then run after it. The first to reach the bottom wins.

What do you think?: open answers

After You Read: 1. B **2.** C **3.** A **4.** D **5.** C **6.** C **7.** A **8.** D **9.** B **10.** A **11.** D **12.** C

Grammar Practice

Intensive Pronouns: **A. 1.** itself **2.** yourself **3.** himself **4.** herself
B. 1. themselves **2.** yourselves **3.** ourselves **4.** themselves
Relative Pronouns: **1.** The *capoeira* master, who is also a mentor, is respected by many. **2.** That martial art, which is called *capoeira*, is also a kind of dance. **3.** Those students, whom Mary knows, go to her school.
Phrasal Verbs: **1.** put on **2.** keep on **3.** fill out **4.** turn off **5.** run after

Video Practice

A. 1. competition **2.** pumpkins **3.** don't **4.** 14 **5.** farthest **B. 1.** teams **2.** the machine **3.** a cannon **4.** refrigerators **5.** breaks **C. 1.** combination **2.** slaves **3.** at risk **4.** homeless **D. 1.** within **2.** of **3.** on **4.** from
E. 1. pushes **2.** enjoy **3.** rolled **4.** crowd **5.** failed **6.** thinks **F. 1.** 1800s **2.** 40 **3.** first **4.** 30 **5.** two

Exit Test

1. C **2.** D **3.** B **4.** C **5.** B **6.** C **7.** C **8.** pumpkins **9.** False **10.** True **11.** C **12.** D **13.** D **14.** A **15.** B **16.** B **17.** B **18.** A **19.** C **20.** A **21.** C **22.** A **23.** C **24.** D **25.** B **26.** C **27.** A **28.** B **29.** D **30.** A

English - Chinese Vocabulary List 中英對照生詞表

(Arranged in alphabetical order)

abolish	廢除	**integrate**	結合
accident	意外	**martial art**	武術
amusement	娛樂	**mentor**	良師
balance	平衡	**microwave**	微波爐
behaviour	行為	**mould**	塑造
bruise	傷痕	**norm**	規範
cannon	大砲	**original**	原創的
catapult	投石機	**participant**	參加的人
considerable	相當多的	**progress**	進步
contraption	機器	**pub**	酒吧
crash barrier	防撞欄	**Punkin' Chunkin'**	拋南瓜
crazy	瘋狂的	**run after**	追逐
drive	驅使	**sacred**	神聖的
drug	毒品	**slave**	奴隸
engineer	設計	**slope**	斜坡
explosive	炸藥	**take out**	破壞
fame	名聲	**tremendous**	極巨大的
foster home	寄養家庭	**unfortunately**	不幸地
get (one's) hands on	(某人)找到的	**vendor**	小販
give up	放棄	**weld**	焊接點
heritage	文化傳統	**what it can take**	這個機器有多強
in charge	負責管理	**widow**	寡婦
injure	受傷		